Learn About

ANIMAL COVERINGS

MW01153564

SCALES

by Eric Geron

Children's Press®
An imprint of Scholastic Inc.

Library of Congress Cataloging-in-Publication Data

Names: Geron, Eric, author.
Title: Scales / by Eric Geron.
Description: First edition. | New York : Children's Press, an imprint of
  Scholastic Inc., 2024. | Series: Learn about: animal coverings |
  Includes index. | Audience: Ages 5–7 | Audience: Grades K–1 | Summary:
  "Let's learn all about the different types of animal coverings! Animals
  have different body coverings for different reasons. Some animals use
  their coverings to keep warm or stay cool, others use them for
  protection, and can either stand out or blend in. Some animals even use
  their coverings to move! This vibrant new set of LEARN ABOUT books gives
  readers a close-up look at five different animal coverings, from fur and
  feathers to skin, scales, and shells. Each book is packed with
  photographs and fun facts that explore how each covering suits the
  habitat, diet, survival, and life cycle of various animals in the
  natural world. Which animals have scales? Fish! Did you know that some
  birds, reptiles, and mammals can also have scales? Discover all the
  incredible ways scales help animals survive. With amazing photos and
  lively text, this book explains how scales help animals stay warm or
  cool, move, protect themselves, and more! Get ready to learn all about
  scales!"—Provided by publisher.
Identifiers: LCCN 2023000501 (print) | LCCN 2023000502 (ebook) |
  ISBN 9781338898057 (library binding) | ISBN 9781338898064 (paperback) |
  ISBN 9781338898071 (ebook)
Subjects: LCSH: Scales (Reptiles)—Juvenile literature. | Scales
  (Fishes)—Juvenile literature. | Body covering (Anatomy)—Juvenile
  literature. | Animal defenses—Juvenile literature. |
  Animals—Adaptation—Juvenile literature. | BISAC: JUVENILE NONFICTION /
  Animals / General | JUVENILE NONFICTION / Science & Nature / General
  (see also headings under Animals or Technology)
Classification: LCC QL942 .G473 2024 (print) | LCC QL942 (ebook) | DDC
  591.47/7—dc23/eng/20230110
LC record available at https://lccn.loc.gov/2023000501
LC ebook record available at https://lccn.loc.gov/2023000502

10 9 8 7 6 5 4 3 2 1   24 25 26 27 28
Printed in China   62

First edition, 2024
Book design by Kay Petronio

Photos ©: 3 bottom right: MarkMirror/Getty Images; 5 inset: imv/Getty Images; 6–7
background: Narongkan Wanchauy/Getty Images; 7 top right: Mark Kostich/Getty Images;
7 top center: Ralf Geithe/Getty Images; 7 bottom center: Ssola/Wikimedia; 7 bottom
right: feathercollector/Getty Images; 8 background left: Abstract Aerial Art/Getty Images;
9 bottom: AppleZoomZoom/Getty Images; 11 top: Cheryl Power/Science Source; 12–13
background: Wirestock/Getty Images; 13 inset: NNStock/Alamy Images; 14 top: Marco
Uliana/Alamy Images; 14 bottom left, 14 bottom right: JasonOndreicka/Getty Images; 16
bottom: Darrell Gulin/Getty Images; 17 main: David Tipling/NPL/Minden Pictures; 17 inset:
Ralf Geithe/Getty Images; 18 inset top: Ken Griffiths/Getty Images; 20 inset: ifish/Getty
Images; 21 inset: Gerald Corsi/Getty Images; 22 bottom left, 22 bottom right: Maarten
Wouters/Getty Images; 23 inset: DurdenImages/Getty Images; 26 inset right: Clouds Hill
Imaging Ltd./Getty Images; 28: Mark Kostich/Getty Images; 29 center left: sdbower/
Getty Images; 29 center right: Photo by marianna armata/Getty Images; 30 top right: etra
Images/Getty Images.

All other photos © Shutterstock.

A special thank-you to the team at the Cincinnati Zoo & Botanical Garden for their expert consultation.

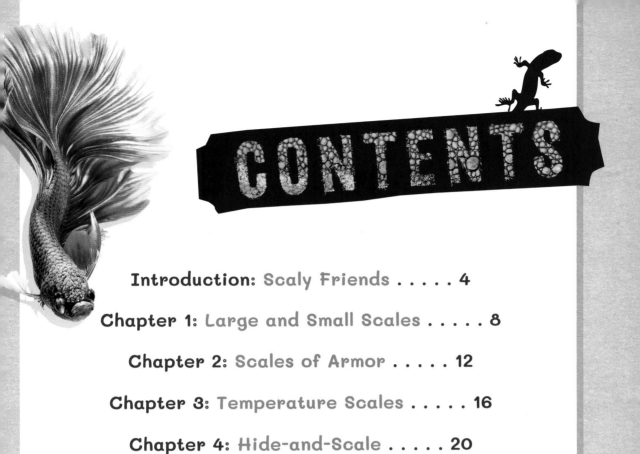

CONTENTS

Scaly Friends

Animal bodies can have different coverings. Some are covered with fur or feathers. Others are covered with shells or skin. Some animals have more than one covering! This book is all about a special covering: **scales**! Scales are little plates that grow out of an animal's skin.

Close-up of
chameleon scales

CHAMELEON

Scales grow in many colors
and patterns. Discover which
animals have them, what scales
are made of, and the amazing things
they can do.

Which Animals Have Scales?

Fish, birds, reptiles, and **arthropods**, like moths and butterflies, are covered in scales. Fish live in the water. Most birds soar through the air. All reptiles have backbones and breathe air. Arthropods have no backbone.

Most dinosaurs were covered in scales!

Birds have scales that cover their legs or feet. Fish, reptiles, and arthropods have scales that cover their entire bodies!

CHAPTER 1
Large and Small Scales

Scales are really useful. Just like there are different types of animals, there are also different types of scales. They can be big or small or pointy or round.

GREEN PIT VIPER

CHAMELEON TAIL

Each type of scale plays an important role. Some scales protect animals against **predators**. Some scales allow animals to control their body temperature. Sometimes scales help animals move.

Crocodiles have big scales called scutes!

SALMON

Scales

This is a salmon. It uses its small scales like a suit of armor to protect itself. All fish scales are covered in slimy **mucus** that helps fish swim smoothly through water. Being covered in slippery scales also makes sure nothing can attach to them.

Salmon are covered in cycloid (SYE-kloid) scales. They are smooth and circular.

Scales also help make fish more flexible. Each scale has growth rings that can tell the age of a fish. The more rings the scales have, the older the fish.

CHAPTER 2

Scales of Armor

Scales protect animals in other ways. The scales on birds' feet act like shoes. Without their scales, birds' feet would get hurt from walking.

PANGOLIN

The only **mammal** whose body is fully covered in scales is the pangolin. They can roll up in a ball. Their hard scales keep them safe from attackers.

Scales can also help an animal escape. If a moth gets caught in a spiderweb, the scales that are stuck will break off.

COMMON COOT

Moth caught in a spiderweb

Warning Scales

The colors of scales do a great job at protecting animals from danger. They warn predators to stay away. Most of the time, colorful scales let predators know their **prey** will not taste good. Butterflies and moths have eyespots on their wings. These marks make attackers aim for the wings instead of their bodies.

MOTH

NONVENOMOUS:
Scarlet Kingsnake

VENOMOUS:
Eastern Coral Snake

Sometimes nonvenomous animals will have the same color scales as **venomous** animals to trick predators.

GREEN BUSH VIPER

Brightly colored scales can also let predators know an animal is venomous. Some reptiles with these kinds of colorful scales include sea snakes, coral snakes, and green bush vipers.

CHAPTER 3

Temperature Scales

Animals use their scales to help control their body temperature by cooling off or warming up. Birds and reptiles are **cold-blooded**. One way birds can keep warm is by using the scales on their feet to trap heat close to their bodies. This allows them to stay warm in the cold.

MOURNING CLOAK

Sometimes the scales on butterflies soak up the sun to give them energy to fly.

IGUANA

SILVER Y MOTH

Reptiles use their scales to warm up, too. They lie in the sun to absorb the heat. Most moths are **nocturnal**. They fly at night, when the temperature is cooler. Because they can't soak up the sun during the day, moths have thick layers of scales to help stay warm.

Cooling Down

Scales can also help animals to keep cool and avoid water loss. The scales prevent them from getting too hot or dried up. Reptile scales prevent water from leaving their bodies.

Reptile scales are made from **keratin**, the same material that makes up fur, nails, and feathers.

BEARDED DRAGON

LEOPARD GECKO

GILA MONSTER

Lizards are reptiles. They only need a small amount of water to live, especially in warm, dry places like a desert. Scales on butterfly wings also keep them cool and dry.

CHAPTER 4

Hide-and-Scale

Many animals have scales that allow them to hide in their **habitat**. This ability to blend into their surroundings is called **camouflage**. It helps protect animals from being seen by predators or prey.

Some fish, like the seahorse, do not have scales at all but can still camouflage.

LEAF-TAILED GECKO

The leaf-tailed gecko vanishes into its surroundings. Its dull, brown scales look like trees and branches. The flounder can disappear because its scales look like part of the ocean floor.

FLOUNDER

Color-Changing Scales

Did you know that the scales in some animals can change from one color to another? Chameleons have scales that can change into many colors. They can change colors in a matter of seconds!

CHAMELEON

Changing colors allows animals to soak up more heat when it's cold out and less heat when it's hot out.

TRUMPETFISH

GREEN FORESTER MOTH

Trumpetfish sneak up on prey by changing colors to blend into the water. The green forester moth is green during the day. It changes to a rusty red in the morning and at night.

CHAPTER 5

What Else Can Scales Do?

Animals use their scales for more than camouflage and temperature control. They can also use them to communicate! Colorful scales can attract mates.

Fish also use the color of their scales to communicate with other fish.

PINEAPPLEFISH

PANTHER CHAMELEON

Chameleons can also use their colorful scales to show how they are feeling. If a chameleon turns darker, it likely feels upset. If it turns a brighter color, it likely feels happy.

Movement

Scales can help animals move from one place to another! Snakes have flat scales on their bellies that grip on to surfaces and help them crawl. Scales on geckos' feet allow them to climb and hold on to smooth surfaces.

Did you know sharks are covered in scales? Their scales are like tiny teeth.

Great white shark scales close-up

Swallowtail butterfly
wing close-up

SWALLOWTAIL
BUTTERFLY

TOKAY GECKO

Butterflies use
the scales on
their wings to
make flying
easier. Air
gets trapped
between their
scales and their
wings. This
trapped air
helps lift their
bodies up.

New Scales

Many animals lose their scales and replace them with a new layer. This is called shedding, or **molting**. Birds molt the scales on their feet. Reptiles shed the scales covering their entire bodies. Fish do not molt. This means as fish grow larger, so do their scales.

Bush viper molting

Chameleon

Brown Anole

Molting gets rid of old scales to allow for newer scales to grow. Reptiles shed to replace old scales with larger scales.

New scales allow animals to stay healthy and survive.

IGUANA

CONCLUSION

GREEN SWALLOWTAIL BUTTERFLY

Scales Matter

Now you know all about scales! They can be colorful and smooth or dull and hard. Animals need them to survive. Scales help animals keep warm, stay cool, warn predators to go away, and hide from view. They can also protect animals from harm. Next time you see a scaly animal, remember how its scales make so many things possible for it.

The reptile with some of the toughest scales is the Komodo dragon!